This book belongs to

....

make believe ideas

Puss in Boots

Key sound short a spellings: a
Secondary sounds: ck, oo, ss

Written by Rosie Greening
Illustrated by Clare Fennell

Reading with phonics

How to use this book

The **Reading with phonics** series helps you to have fun with your child and to support their learning of phonics and reading. It is aimed at children who have learned the letter sounds and are building confidence in their reading.

Each title in the series focuses on a different key sound or blend of sounds. The entertaining retelling of the story repeats this sound frequently, and the different spellings for the sound or blend of sounds are highlighted in red type. The first activity at the back of the book provides practice in reading and using words containing this sound or blend of sounds. The key sound for **Puss in Boots** is **short a.**

Start by reading the story to your child, asking them to join in with the refrain in bold. Next, encourage them to read the story with you. Give them a hand to decode tricky words.

Now look at the activity pages at the back of the book. These are intended for you and your child to enjoy together. Most are not activities to complete in pencil or pen, but by reading and talking or pointing.

The **Key sound** pages focus on one sound, and on the various different groups of letters that produce that sound. Encourage your child to read the different letter groups and complete the activity, so they become more aware of the variety of spellings there are for the same sound.

The **Letters together** pages look at three pairs or groups of letters and at the sounds they make as they work together. Help your child to read the words and trace the route on the word maps.

Rhyme is used a lot in these retellings. Whatever stage your child has reached in their learning of phonics, it is always good practice for them to listen carefully for sounds and find words that rhyme. The pages on **Rhyming words** take six words from the story and ask children to read and find other words that rhyme with them.

The **Key words** pages focus on a number of key words that occur regularly but can nonetheless be challenging. Many of these words are not sounded out following the rules of phonics and the easiest thing is for children to learn them by sight, so that they do not worry about decoding them. These pages encourage children to retell the story, practising key words as they do so.

The **Picture dictionary** page asks children to focus closely on nine words from the story. Encourage children to look carefully at each word, cover it with their hand, write it on a separate piece of paper, and finally, check it!

Do not complete all the activities at once – doing one each time you read will ensure that your child continues to enjoy the stories and the time you are spending together. **Have fun!**

Three sons were given news one day –
their mean old dad had passed away.
He'd left some cash for Sam and Pat,
but Dan just got his father's cat.

Dan has an amazing cat.
But he wants cash like Sam and Pat!

"I'm not a fan of cats," Dan said.
"I want some stacks of cash instead!"
The cat said, "I can help you there.
But first, I want new shoes to wear."

Young Dan was poor – he needed gold!
And so he did as he was told.
He bought a brand-new swanky hat
and matching boots for Puss the cat.

Dan has an amazing cat.
He buys him shoes and a new hat!

The cat said, "Right! I have a plan
to turn you into one rich man.
Our first act is to send the King
a bag of all his favourite things!"

8

Puss filled a bag with juicy ham,
some apples and big jars of jam.
He signed the tag: "With love from Dan –
a very nice and handsome man."

FROM DAN

Dan has an amazing cat.
They send a ham that's big and fat!

The gift from Dan made King Jack smile.
He said, "Wowee! This man has style."

The king sent back a thank-you note:
"Please visit anytime!" he wrote.

Dan has an amazing cat.
Puss has a plan that won't fall flat!

"Let's carry on!" the sly cat cried,
and led Dan to the riverside.
He ordered Dan to swim around,
then hid his clothes without a sound.

12

Before too long, King Jack passed by.
The cat dashed up and gave a cry:
"A man has robbed the handsome Dan –
you have to help him, if you can!"

Dan has an amazing cat.
He asks for help in seconds flat!

13

"I'd love to help him," cried the King.
"That man sent all my favourite things."
He handed Dan a brand-new suit,
a carriage and a snack to boot!

The cat told Dan, "That went as planned.
But now you need a house that's grand."
So Puss ran to a mansion home,
where Matt the ogre lived alone.

NO
TRESPASSING!

Dan has an amazing cat.
Puss goes to visit Ogre Matt.

This ogre could turn into things,
like animals or birds with wings.
Said Puss, "I'll trick him if I can,
and hand this mansion straight to Dan!"

Puss banged the door, and out came Matt.
"Let's play a game," declared the cat.
"If I name something you can't be,
you have to give your house to me."

16

Dan has an amazing cat.
The cat and Matt begin to chat.

17

The ogre laughed, "I'll play with you,
but there is nothing I can't do."

The cat said, "Can you be a bat?"
and Matt transformed in seconds flat.

The cat said, "I'm amazed, it's true.
But can you be a camel, too?"
The ogre changed and shouted, "See?
There's nothing that I cannot be!"

Dan has an amazing cat.
He plays a trick on Ogre Matt.

"I've got it!" said the crafty cat.
"I bet you can't become a rat."
But when he did, Puss gave a grin:
he pounced on Matt and swallowed him!

The magic ogre was no more,
so Puss wrote "Dan's house" on the door.
King Jack arrived and was impressed.
He shouted, "Dan, you are the best!"

Dan has an amazing cat.

Puss gobbles up that little rat!

The King set Dan up with young Clare,
his daughter, who was smart and fair.
So Dan was happy after that,
all thanks to Puss, his clever cat!

Dan has an amazing cat,
and now Dan's rich, so that is that!

Key sound

There are other groups of letters that make the short a sound. Practise them by following the different short a coins to help Puss buy a new hat. Start with the a words, and then have a go at the ai and i words in the purple coins.

cat

plan

pat

man

hat

an

quack

plaid

plait

snack

bat

that

rat

clap

flat

cap

fat

ran

apple

bag

camel

meringue

dad

25

Letters together

Look at these pairs of letters and say the sounds they make.

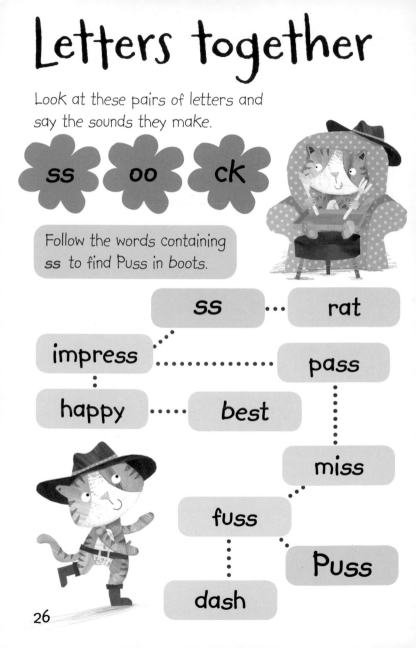

ss   **oo**   **ck**

Follow the words containing *ss* to find Puss in boots.

ss · · · rat

impress · · · · · · · · · · · pass

happy · · · · best

miss

fuss

Puss

dash

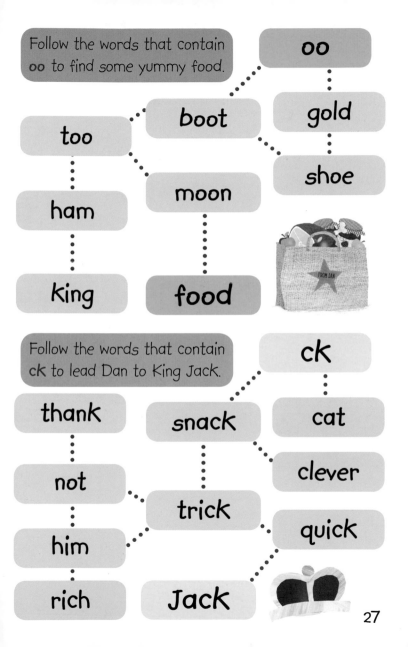

Follow the words that contain **oo** to find some yummy food.

oo

boot — gold

too — shoe

ham — moon

king — **food**

Follow the words that contain **ck** to lead Dan to King Jack.

ck

thank — snack — cat

not — clever

him — trick — quick

rich — Jack

Rhyming words

Read and say the words in the flowers and then point to other words that rhyme with them.

| hat | cat | rat |
| house | | and |

| young | boot | hoot |
| root | | shoe |

| clever | mess | guess |
| dress | | puss |

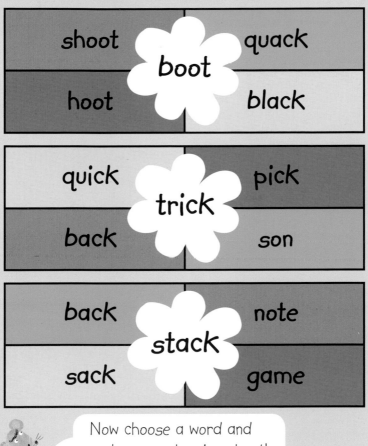

shoot · quack · **boot** · hoot · black

quick · pick · **trick** · back · son

back · note · **stack** · sack · game

Now choose a word and make up a rhyming chant!

Puss is **quick** to **pick** a **trick**!

Key words

Many common words can be tricky to sound out. Practise them by reading these sentences about the story. Now make more sentences using other key words from around the border.

Dan got **his** father's cat.

Puss said he would **make** Dan rich.

He sent King Jack a **big** bag of food.

The gift **made** King Jack smile.

not • your • asked • his • he

• said • very • a • big • had • made • day • off • on •

Puss told the King that Dan **had** been robbed.

The King was happy to **help** Dan.

Puss played a trick **on** the ogre.

Dan moved **into** the ogre's mansion.

King Jack was impressed **by** Dan.

her • saw • in • then • make • the • called • look • by • about • up • you • they • go

old • help • like • into • of • with • was • to

Picture dictionary

Look carefully at the pictures and the words.
Now cover the words, one at a time.
Can you remember how to write them?

bag

boots

camel

carriage

cash

cat

mansion

ogre

swim